FOR MORGAN'S GRANDPA

PAT HUTCHINS

NIGHT

Aladdin Paperbacks

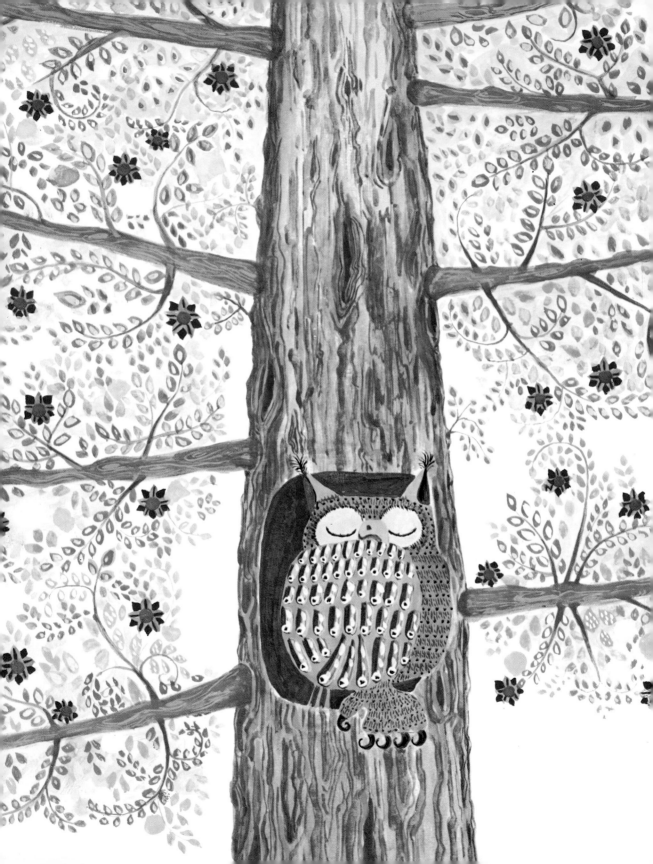

Owl tried to sleep.

The bees buzzed,
buzz buzz,
and Owl tried to sleep.

The squirrel cracked nuts,
crunch crunch,
and Owl tried to sleep.

The crows croaked,
caw caw,
and Owl tried to sleep.

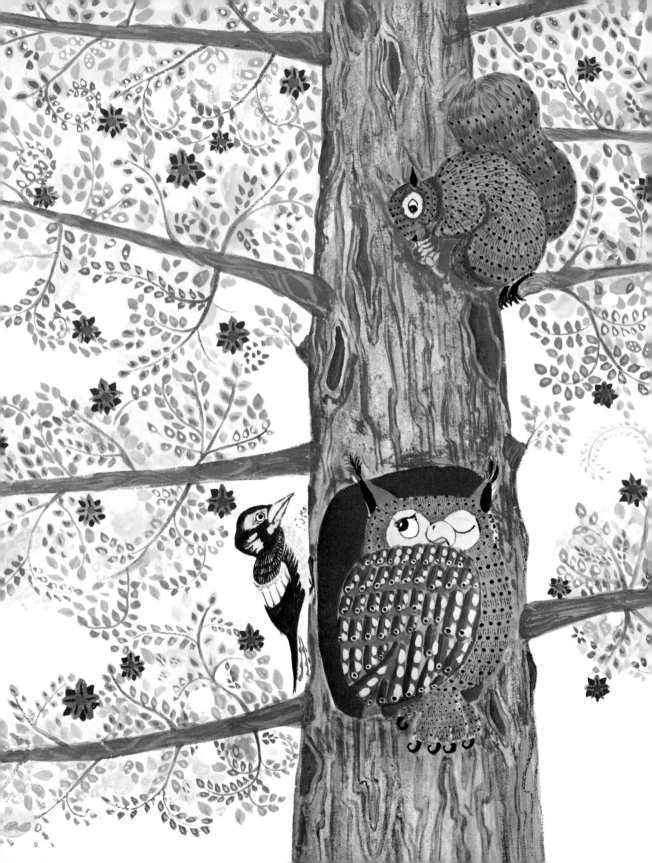

The woodpecker pecked,
rat-a-tat! rat-a-tat!
and Owl tried to sleep.

The starlings chittered,
twit-twit, twit-twit,
and Owl tried to sleep.

The jays screamed,
ark ark,
and Owl tried to sleep.

The cuckoo called,
cuckoo cuckoo,
and Owl tried to sleep.

The robin peeped,
pip pip,
and Owl tried to sleep.

The sparrows chirped,
cheep cheep,
and Owl tried to sleep.

The doves cooed,
croo croo,
and Owl tried to sleep.

The bees buzzed, buzz buzz.
The squirrel cracked nuts,
crunch crunch.
The crows croaked, caw caw.
The woodpecker pecked,
rat-a-tat! rat-a-tat!
The starlings chittered,
twit-twit, twit-twit.
The jays screamed, ark ark.
The cuckoo called,
cuckoo cuckoo.
The robin peeped, pip pip.
The sparrows chirped,
cheep cheep.
The doves cooed, croo croo,
and Owl couldn't sleep.

Then darkness fell
and the moon came up.
And there wasn't a sound.

Owl screeched,
screech screech,
and woke everyone up.

Aladdin Paperbacks
An imprint of Simon & Schuster
Children's Publishing Division
1230 Avenue of the Americas
New York, NY 10020

First Aladdin Paperbacks edition, 1990
Printed in the United States of America
A hardcover edition of *Good-Night, Owl!* is available from
Simon & Schuster Books for Young Readers

15   14   13   12   11   10   9   8

Library of Congress Cataloging-in-Publication Data
Hutchins, Pat, 1942–
Good-night, owl! / Pat Hutchins.   p.   cm.
Reprint. Originally published: New York: Macmillan, 1972.
Summary: Because all the other animals' noises keep him from
sleeping, Owl watches for a chance to take his revenge.
ISBN 0-689-71371-1
1. Owls—Juvenile fiction. 2. Animals—Juvenile fiction.
[1. Owls—Fiction. 2. Animals—Fiction] I. Title.
PZ103H969Go 1990
[E]—dc20   89-17708   CIP   AC